Richard H. Wilmer, Virginia F. Boyle

Brokenburne

a southern auntie's war tale, by Virginia Frazer Boyle

Richard H. Wilmer, Virginia F. Boyle

Brokenburne
a southern auntie's war tale, by Virginia Frazer Boyle

ISBN/EAN: 9783337089153

Printed in Europe, USA, Canada, Australia, Japan

Cover: Foto ©Andreas Hilbeck / pixelio.de

More available books at **www.hansebooks.com**

BROKENBURNE

A SOUTHERN AUNTIE'S WAR TALE

BY

VIRGINIA FRAZER BOYLE

WITH ILLUSTRATIONS BY WM. HENRY WALKER

NEW YORK
E. R. HERRICK & COMPANY
1897

THE DE VINNE PRESS.

LIST OF ILLUSTRATIONS

TO MY MOTHER

BROKENBURNE.

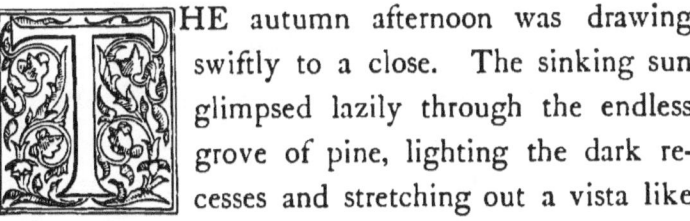HE autumn afternoon was drawing swiftly to a close. The sinking sun glimpsed lazily through the endless grove of pine, lighting the dark recesses and stretching out a vista like a vast enchanted hall of colonnades.

Along the beach road slowly through the heavy sand toiled two tired travelers on horseback. The one, evidently Southern born, was cicerone and guide, and was revisiting familiar scenes and places after a long absence. The other, a young Northerner, was making a tour of novelty through, to him, a hitherto undiscovered country.

"Let me see," exclaimed the cicerone. "The old Balfour place must be about here somewhere. I remember it as a child before we moved to Tennessee. Our presence at that gate is all the introduction we need, Frank. I have heard my father speak of them often. Gentlefolks of the old school, chivalry and all that sort of thing; they were handsome entertainers before the war."

"Before the war!—everything was before the war,—not in the year of our Lord so and so, but before or after the war, as I fancy Noah's people must have said 'after the deluge'!"

"See, this must be the road; we 'll risk it at any rate," and Clem turned sharply into a broad untraveled road or lane, Frank dreamily following.

"Yes, there is the place!" cried Clem, as a massive white outline rose from amongst a grove of liveoak. "I knew that my childish impressions would not deceive me!"

The place was a typical old Southern home of which it had been said that the latch-string hung upon the outside and no one touched it twice ere it was opened.

Not a human thing seemed astir; over the arching gateway the rose-vines swayed in the evening breeze, and bee and butterfly made merry amid the foliage, loth to be driven from Arcadia, even by the coming darkness. Roses, roses everywhere; the

Maréchal Niel laying its yellow head upon the breast of the wild Cherokee, the rose of love kissing the pale cheek of the white La Marque. Roses, roses everywhere, hiding unsightly gaps, holding up the rotting arch, a tribute still to pride, covering up the poverty of decaying grandeur.

"Things have gone fearfully to rack — poor, proud old place," said Clem, regretfully, as the great old gate swung creaking behind them.

"Yes, yes, but what a subject for a painter!" cried Frank, enthusiastically.

"What a subject for a moralist — a fatalist, if you will," said the other, solemnly.

Softly the old knocker was lifted and dropped, waking strange echoes in the hall beyond.

"I am afraid that we shall spend the night in the woods," said Clem, ruefully; "the folks must all be away, and have been gone for a long time too," he added, looking upon the grass-grown walk.

"No, no, Clem, only your dreamy Southern way of doing things — did n't I tell you so?" as a turbaned head peered from around the corner of the house, ere a small black figure appeared, bearing in her hands an enormous bunch of keys.

"I 'se sorry I ain't hear you at de gate," she said,

in evident embarrassment, nervously smoothing her snowy apron and eyeing keenly the faces of the young men. "But howsome-ebber, I gibs de welcome er de place ter young Marse's gues's. I 'se sorry he ain't home at de present, but maybe you done brung me er word fum him," said the old woman, making as though she would unlock the door, but still delaying the action.

Gradually the situation was explained and the Northern friend formally introduced.

"I 'se glad ter meet your frien', sar," she said, fairly beaming with hospitality, "but you don' mean ter say dat you is leetle Clemmie, Marse Clem Ledgerwood's leetle Clemmie? I means you was when I seed you las'," as the great brawny man smiled.

"Yes, I 'm Clemmie," said he, stretching out his long tired legs.

"Lord! don' I 'member Marse Clem, dough! him an' ole Marse was des lack brudders!" and, briskly unlocked, the great door swung wide. "Up an' maired er leetle gal in ole De Soty an' fotch her home, all unbeknownst ter anybody, don't I 'member!" Busily she dusted the stiff old damask chairs and opened the drawing-room windows.

Her unexpected visitors remained smoking on the

verandah, undecided, undetermined what to do, certainly not feeling very comfortable. Now, flustered and important, the old woman stood in the doorway. " Ole Bene make you welcome ter Brokenburne. Hit do her proud ter sarve young Marse's gues's."

" Is the family away, Aunt Bene?" ventured Clem, anxious for information without displaying his ignorance.

" Young Marse am 'way, but we 'spec's him home mos' any time,— mought be here ter-night, maybe."

" Where is Colonel Balfour?"

" Ole Marse done dead an' gone, lo! dese many years," she said, reverently.

"And the Madame?"

" Dead too."

" There was a daughter?"

" Miss Jinny,— but dar hain't nobody lef' ter Brokenburne but young Marse; we 'spec's him home mos' any time."

" Ury! Jule!" she shouted, awaking to a sense of hospitality as two ragged little negroes made their appearance. " Take de gemmen's hosses roun' ter de stable, an' min' you feeds an' rubs 'em well too! Marse Clemmie an' young Marse, de vally show

1*

you ter your rooms ter-rectly," and with a smile and courtesy she was gone.

"Clem," muttered Frank, watching the soft blue veil float dreamily from his fragrant Havana, "you don't seem to know any more about the present than I do."

"No, it is all traditionary with me. There is a mystery about it I wish I could solve."

"Do you think that it is perfectly safe here?" queried Frank, rising in mock alarm. "I doubt it!" as a thumping sound was heard at the other end of the long hall. Slowly through the dusk it came, nearer and nearer; then the white-haired figure bowed so low it raised itself with difficulty.

"I 'nounce de tea ter-rectly, sar; sarve you ter your rooms, sar." Poor shadow of an ebon Chesterfield! Thy hospitable memories awake; thy poor legs feel the nimble impulse of courtly servitude, but nature says you nay. Thy stock and waistcoat both well served thy master's sire in his time, and now it serveth thee to help preserve thy house's name in the hour of need!

"I 'nounce de tea shortly, sar, sarve you ter your rooms, sar!"

Who else, but ole Marse's valet!

"I feel like a child with too much of fairy stories," said Frank, laving his face in the cool soft water; then gazing on the scene of old-time elegance around him, "everything in its place as though it were used yesterday, and how well preserved, enchanted, as it were."

"Yes," said the other, "but it seems odder to you than to me."

"I believe that you are under a spell too," laughed Frank, his eyes fixed upon the portrait of a fair young girl, hanging over the mantel.

Again the echoing "thump, thump," and the door was flung open and held by the old serving-man in his faded livery.

"Tea am sarved!" he announced in blandest tones, with another stately bow.

"All right," said the young Southerner as spokesman, still hesitating to accept the hospitality, to eat the salt of a man under such circumstances, mysterious circumstances, for the house evidently had not been in general use for a number of years.

"Will you show us down, Uncle —?"

"Aaron, at your sarvice, sar!" said that functionary, with great unction.

Once in the broad hall old Aaron unbent from his rigid formality and even grew garrulous.

"I 'se powerful 'feared you git lonesome here, gemmen, wid de young Marse 'way, but we 'spec's him home mos' any day now, an' we makes you welcome ter Brokenburne."

"Lack ter hunt?" he inquired, when the party had expressed their thankful appreciation.

"We got guns an' hosses. Dey putty ole, but ole t'ings is de bes', 'ca'se dey don' mek t'ings now as good as dey usen to; but dorgs, Lord! you oughter see our dorgs,—whoopee!—de breed kin—" but the frowning face and uplifted finger of Bene through the dining-room door suddenly checked the balmy flow of small talk, and gravely and silently he bowed the gentlemen in to supper—a supper worthy, however, of minute description. Above the dainty damask, wafting faintly the lavender and rosemary of the linen-chest, gleamed the exquisite china and ancient service of the Balfours, awakening from their long sleep to look upon the massive candelabra and to reflect a myriad of sputtering tallow dips. At the head of the oaken table, behind the silver urn, stood the smiling Bene. There was country hospitality galore. Chicken, fried a golden brown, big fat comfortable

biscuit, buttermilk and eggbread; and boyish appe-
tites, hesitating no longer, "set to" with a will.

"I never drank such coffee as this before," exclaimed Frank, watching the fragrant fluid pouring
for the second or third time upon the matchless
cream.

"Maybe you wa'n't borned in de Souf, honey —
dis am real Soufern coffee." Aunt Bene smiled
complacently. "Ole Miss hab hit on her table des
lack dis fur forty year an' nebber fail onct. Lord!
ef ole Miss' coffee *'pear* ter fail, um!"—and Aunt
Bene looked around nervously.

"I 'se sorry, gemmen, powerful sorry, dey hain't no
wine in de cellar," said Uncle Aaron, poising his silver
waiter; "leastways, not ter-night; de war dreen ever'
kaig uv 'em, but young Marse done order some fum
N'Orleans. Maybe hit git here ter-morrer."

Another ominous glance from Bene, and, being
assured that it was not needed, Aaron relapsed into
silence again.

"Aunt Bene," said Clem, when the hearty meal
had been finished, "we have enjoyed our supper
very much; we shall have to take breakfast with
you, and we want to do our part of the providing."

"Lord, young Marse!" exclaimed Aunt Bene, recoiling from the money in acute distress and mortification, "I hain't er-lettin' lodgin's! I 'sten' ter young Marse's gues's de horsepitality er de house while he erway; you is young Marse's frien's an' you hain't gwine pay nuffin' here!"

"I beg your pardon, Aunt Bene; I did n't understand," said Clem,— an apology in which Frank joined.

"I nebber wuked for no snack house in all my borned days," said Aaron, bristling for the honor of the house. "I hain't no eye-sarvent! Young Marse here ter-day an' gone ter-morrow, I sarve on des de same. I make young Marse's gues's comferble twel he come. I take 'em ter de lodge, I shows 'em de guns, de hosses, de dorgs. Dat breed —." A glance from Bene and the pedigree was never told.

"Well, we 'll see them all to-morrow, Uncle Aaron," said Frank.

"Will de gemmens go arter breakfast, er rise ter de huntin'-horn?" asked Uncle Aaron, with an impressive bow.

"By the horn, by all means," assented both.

Good-nights were exchanged, and the echoing thump preceded them to their chamber. At the door Aaron paused, looked anxiously around, then whispered in Clem's ear: "De breed er dem dorgs is powerful."

There was a faint mustiness in the snowy bed-clothing they drew about them, hardly the odor of decay, but an atmosphere of ancient elegance. What busy head and hands had superintended the stitching of those dainty hems, the weaving of those fabrics, old, most likely, ere these their guests were born?

Hardly had they slept, they thought, when the winding of the hunter's horn broke on their hearty slumbers.

"Clem," cried Frank, "am I dreaming? Have I dropped into the romance of a Scottish tale? Am I summoned to an English meet? Am I in an enchanted wood? Or has old Aaron just hoodooed me?"

"You are in for it now; you had better go and see," laughed the other. "But Frank," he added seriously, "don't laugh at anything that we may see or hear, however ridiculous it may appear; these circumstances are really mysterious and pathetic. We must try to get at the bottom of this for the sake of the old friendship, and see if anything can be done."

Again the winding horn, and old Aaron in full regalia, to which he had added a battered plug hat, stood at the great door, surrounded by a troop of yelping, whining curs.

"Down Pluto! Down Phisto!" he cried, popping at them with a tiny hazel switch.

"Did n't t'ink, gemmen, as how you mought want ter go huntin' dis mornin'," he said, apologetically. "But we mought make ready fur ter-morrer."

Frank and Clem, remembering their compact, repressed in vain the desire to laugh.

"Glad ter fin' you so peart an' lackly dis mornin', gemmen. Good sleep am er mighty good t'ing," said Uncle Aaron, joining good-naturedly in the laugh. "I did n't 'ten' de huntin' in ole Marse's time, Jim do; I b'long ter de house, but ole Aaron do his bestes' fur young Marse's gues's. Haw! haw!"

"We mos'ly rin rabbits dese days. Now Pluto he de bestes' rabbit dorg, but he ain't no quality dorg; he des my dorg, nigger dorg."

The lodge was a kind of office, single story, containing one room, such as was built in antebellum times on each side of the dwelling-house, and was prepared for the reception of male visitors, who were

wont to flock in great numbers for hunting and holiday.

"Here am de guns an' de saddles," said old Aaron, unlocking the door. "Hain't hab no huntin' in er duration, leastways not sence de war; do need ilein' an' sech putty bad," as he ruefully peered down a rusty barrel after vainly trying to raise the hammer.

"Gwine w'ar dat Jim plum inter er frazzle," he added, hotly. (Jim had been dead of old age these ten years gone.) "Young Marse kim home maybe ter-day, an' won't dar be er row!"

Being assured that they really did not care to hunt that day, Uncle Aaron then led them to examine the saddles. Here was the lumbering one of the father, of ancient make, as mouldy as the grave; the lighter one of his hunter son; the remnant of one, tiny and dainty, into which had probably sprung the light form of the young Virginia; here, too, were spurs of silver, steel, and brass.

"Hain't no use tryin' ter do nuffin' wid Jim," grunted Aaron in much mortification. "Young Marse kim dough, an' whoop him up, maybe ter-day. Young Marse mighty keerful an' mighty rich," he added. "See all dat ar lan'? — all dat young Marse's."

"How many acres have you, Uncle Aaron?" asked Frank. Uncle Aaron scratched his head. "Well, I don' know, sar, perzackly, sar, but dar 's powerful many!"

Poor proud Aaron! he forgot to tell that the main part of the land had long been sold for taxes, that the tax on the home had been paid by the honest, earnest endeavors of Bene and himself, against young Marse's final home-coming.

"Now I gwine show you er quality dorg." Through the broad yard limped Aaron toward the dilapidated stables, followed by the young men, upon whom the full pathos of the situation had not yet dawned.

"Prince! h-e-r-e, Prince!" called Aaron, but no response. "He er leetle deef, gemmen, but mighty peart."

Around the corner of the stable came a feeble whine, and a pair of deer hounds, magnificent in their prime, now sightless and toothless, fawned upon another Caleb Balderstone.

Clem's eyes filled; the warm Southern heart was touched. He could understand the devastation that the other knew not of.

"Hain't dey beauties, sar?" and Aaron fondled

the shapely heads. "Dey 's er leetle deef, an' maybe
er leetle blin', and dey 's ole; young Marse gwine
sen' ernudder pack, maybe ter-day, 'ca'se he hatter hab
his dorgs, but Lord! sar, de breed er dese is powerful!"

In like manner and with like results the stables
were viewed, poor old Aaron in his eager recital fail-
ing to see the moved expression upon the faces of
both the young men.

"Here, gemmen," said he, trembling with the
greatness of his information, "I shows you er hoss
dat young Marse excused twenty t'ousan' dollar
fur! Nebber been plowed er worked in his life;
borned and bred in Kaintuck he was!"

"When?" asked Frank, his irrepressible humor
getting the better of him. "Maybe I would like to
buy him."

"Lord, honey!" cried the horror-stricken Aaron.
"*Buy him?* I don' know when he kim, sar, but de
money hain't digged dat 'll buy dat hoss! Did n't
he beat Misser Tripp's Blue Jim an' take de blue
ribbon on all de stakes five year come Christmas
'fore de breakin' out er de war? Money could n't
buy dat hoss, sar!"

"Where is Mr. Tripp now?" queried Frank.

"Dead."

"And Blue Jim?"

"Dead too," said Jack, reverently, taking off his hat out of respect to the racing qualities of the horse, rather than to the nobility of the master.

The sound of the breakfast bell fell pleasantly upon the youthful ears, half glad yet half reluctant to be rid of the painful recital, the struggle of the old Southern pride, which descended as a legacy to the old slave along with his master's old clothes.

"Don' you min' what Bene say; Bene sorter soured," and Aaron brought up the rear, followed by the whinneying old horse, now in a lamentable state of equine dotage.

The hearty breakfast over, preparations were made for a speedy departure, in spite of old Aaron's pleadings to "des stop twel young Marse kim home, he sho' be home soon," when the lowering cloud that had threatened throughout the early morning broke forth in watery wrath. Of course travel was not possible, and not half sorry, the travelers turned into the house, much to the joy of old Aaron and the hospitable Bene.

Having the privilege of the house, they roamed through the great rooms like restless spirits. Here were old pieces of furniture, a harp of exquisite

workmanship among them, rare and quaint enough
to run an "antique maniac" wild. There were por-
traits and unfinished pieces of woman's handiwork,
about which were many theories and conjectures.

But alas! even Paradise shut in would become
wearisome to a man on a rainy day, and soon the
mystery and silence palled upon them.

"I wish I could get to the bottom of this," said
Clem, dreamily running his fingers over the keys of
the rattling old piano.

"Do it; ask the old auntie," said the practical
Frank. "Providence has laid the story right to
your ears, and you are too Southern to take advan-
tage of it," he said, laughing.

So old Bene was sought and traced through the
dining-room, corridors, kitchen, and, her morning
labor over, finally found peacefully carding in her
cabin.

"I makes young Marse's gues's welcome ter my
po' house," she said hastily rising in confusion.
"You did n' git lonesome in de big house by yourse'fs, did you?" she queried kindly, peeping over
her great brass spectacles.

"Well, yes, we did," said Clem, smiling, "and we
thought that we would look you up."

2

"Hit 's been er long time sence de young folkes kim ter ole Bene's cabin,—my kin'er folkes, I mean," she added quickly.

"I uster tell young Marse tales, settin' right here in dis ole hick'ry cheer, many 's de time, many 's de time!"

"Suppose you tell us one, Aunt Bene," said Frank.

"Lord, Lord, he were er baby den!" laughed Bene. "Dat were 'fore we hab any 'flictions, er war, er trouble er nuffin'. Dat war hit were de beginnin' uv hit. Hit bruk up lots er de quality people an sot de niggers free, but hit nebber done no good, fur hit kilt some mighty good white folkes. Dey was des high quality an' could n' stan' hit, an' dey hain't no nigger libin', leastways, I dun know none, dat wa'n't better off bond dan free. But I 'se ole an' po'; I dun know nuffin'," she added cautiously.

"How did it begin, Aunt Bene?" asked Clem, beguiling her into unwariness.

"Ole Marse were dat high quality, an' Aaron, dat po' ole worfless nigger Aaron, you would n' b'leeve hit, young Marse, but he des lack him. He! he! Oh! my law! When I maired Aaron, he were des so lack ole Marse, you could n' er tole 'em, 'cepin' Aaron were black. Dat nigger been er-mawkin' uv ole Marse sence he were free year ole: he walk lack him, he talk lack him, 'cepin' Aaron talk nigger an' ole Marse talk quality, an' he 'clar' he thote perzackly lack ole Marse."

" Well, how did it begin, the war and the trouble, you know," asked Frank, a little impatiently.

" Well, dat 's hit," said Bene, lowering her voice. "Dat Aaron he do be so lack ole Marse, an' ole Marse he keep hisse'f ter hisse'f, an' Aaron say dat er 'oman am er power ter talk, an' he try so hard fur ter make t'ings lack dey uster was."

"But I am a friend of the family, as my father was, and I should like so much to know something of them," said Clem with a quiver in his voice.

" I hain't no han' ter talk 'bout fambly 'fairs, 'ca'se how I lub 'em Gord he know!" and the old voice trembled. " But maybe I kin talk ter dey frien's, an' maybe dey frien's kin tell me 'bout young Marse. We 's er-watchin' an' er-waitin' fur him, but we cain't make t'ings lack dey uster was!"

Old Bene wiped her eyes and looked long and silently into the fire, and she was not interrupted.

We was er mighty happy fambly here, mighty happy. Dar were ole Marse an' ole Miss an' young

Marse an' Miss Jinny who were de baby, an' all de niggers. Niggers! Why, honey, dar was er hundud ter wait on ever' member er de fambly, an' er whole passel lef' ober!

Well, we was all mighty happy. Ole Miss say sometime dat we mos' too happy, dat de Lord lettin' we-all eat de white loaf now, dat we all mought pay mo' 'tention ter dem wha' eaten dey ashcake wid dey tears. Ole Miss she were high up, make er de fines' er de yeth, des bar'ly tech her foot ter de groun' fur er res'in'-place; but ole Marse an' we-all don' pay no 'tention, we des happy, dat all.

Young Marse, he were han'some an' brave an' des es strong! an' Miss Jinny, bress her baby heart! — fur she were my baby, — her were des beau'ful!

Young Marse, he were fair lack he Maw, an' he done growed er leetle mushtache wid er leetle red in hit, got de sperrit uv he Maw. But Miss Jinny, — Gord lub her! — she lack her Paw, so lovin', so sof', so good ter ever't'ing, wid her long brown curls dat git dey red fum de sun, an' big brown eyes lack her ha'r, dat makes you mos' cry when you looks in 'em.

When she leetle, she allus comin' ter me, an' "Mammy," she say, "what I do wid dis po' mouse

dat break his laig in de trap?" An' "Mammy,"
she say, "Ole Puss des whup dis kitten 'ca'se hit
ugly an' po'!"—an' she make er funul fur de mouse,
an' cry her putty eyes red an' nuss dat ole po' cat,
twel she make me mos' crazy. She allus gibin'
close ter de leetle niggers, an' ever' pickaninny on
de place follers her lack er dorg, twel I hatter beat
'em off. She say, "Mammy, dey needs dis, an'
Mammy, dey needs dat," an' one Christmas she
goes ter town wid her Maw an' ups an' buys ever'
pickaninny uv 'em er fine white cambric hankercher.

Well, I watches her grow ter be mos' er 'oman,
an' I lubs ever' bone in her body, but I oneasy in my
min' 'bout her, 'ca'se dar was cu'i's t'ings happin w'en
her was borned.

Ole Miss she were sech er high flyer, an' hab so
much comp'ny an' were so busy, dat we ain' bodder
her wid de leetle troubles er-growin', but we des let
her show us off, an' she dat proud, Lordy! So I
were er mudder ter her, er mudder lack po' white
chillun hab, wha' got time ter lis'en ter 'em laugh an'
hear 'em cry too, an' hain't got no larnin' ter talk
erbout.

Miss Jinny she wa'n't ebber stout, an' hit 'pear lack
de harder we lubs her an' de mo' we ties on ter her,

2*

de mo' lack er piece er fine chiny she git. Ole
Marse's eyes dey fills when he look at her an' he call
her he "Sunbeam," but ole Miss she makin' ready
fur ter make er fine lady uv her, 'ca'se she putty nigh
growed.

Dey hain't no mo' leetle apuns fur Mammy ter
button, er leetle white toes fur Mammy ter tie up,
'ca'se de Baby don' go b'arfooted no mo'.

Well, one summer young Marse kim home fum
college an' fotch he mate, wha' were young Marse
Philip Le Grand, an' lib nigh here, an' dat done de
t'ing fur we-all. Ole Marse he don' lack hit, but he
sorter laugh an' say sumpen 'bout "puppy lub,"—
dat all.

Den anudder summer he kim home wid young
Marse an' when he lef' he caired one er de Baby's
long curls wid him, an' dey writ,—'ca'se she read dem
letters ter her ole Mammy.

He were des er-lubin' her es hard es ebber he
could, an' de putty color kim er-creepin' an' creepin'
up, an' dem long lashes would drap, when she came
ter dat putty white folkes' lub talk.

He were smart an' he were rich an' he writ lack er
man. He were han'some es er pictur, too, but I
lacks er eye dat you kin look plum frough, an' see

de Gord's truf at de bottom, an' Marse Phil hain't got
dat eye; maybe hit were de furrin blood, but I hain't
unnerstan' him.

I set wid de Baby ever' night an' comb out de
long curls fur her, 'ca'se she won't let anybody do hit
but her Mammy; an' she shet de do' an' take er pictur fum roun' her nake, an' look at hit fur er long
time, whilst I er-combin' out de curls. Den she take
dis ole chin twixt her putty white fingers an' say,
"Mammy, hain't he manly, hain't he han'some, hain't
he brave? Dar nuffin' on dis yeth dat he would n'
do fur your Baby!" Den she bring her face nigher
an' she whisper, "An' I gwine be his leetle wife some
day." Den she say, "Mammy, does you lub him?
Say you lubs him des er leetle, Mammy, now
Mammy, please Mammy!" an' she tease me so, I
hatter say I lubs him des er leetle, dough de Marster
furgibe me fur de lie den!

"T'ings is gittin' on mighty fas', " I says ter myse'f,
says I, fur de Baby ride ever' day ter de pos'-orfice
herse'f, an' when she git er letter she sing all day, an'
when one ain't come, she go by herse'f an' play an'
play on de harp twel hit des talk an' moan out'n
sorrer.

Bein' as how I were de mudder, I feels I has er

call ter up an' 'sult wid ole Miss. Ole Miss she set
proud lack an' 'pear lack she git sorter mad; hearts
an' sech lack yethly t'ings were 'way down unner ole
Miss's foot. An' she say, " Bene, you allus worryin'
dat chile an' yourse'f, too, 'bout sumpen ruther.
Course people gwine lub my chile, in course many
luvyers gwine seek her, an' when de time come, she
make er mairge ter er 'vantage, dat 's fitten ter her
birf. You let her 'lone, dis des er notion. All young
gals do dat way, but hit w'ar off. My darter hain't
ebber mairey er Le Grand ! "

I hain't got no call ter say no mo', 'ca'se I don'
wanter bodder ole Marse.

Den kim times dat you don' know nuffin' 'bout,
young Marse, when war hanged ober us lack er big
brack cloud dat would n' bust, an' would n' cl'ar yit,
but des grumble an' grumble an' growl an' growl.
Some folkes did n' b'leeve we gwine hab hit, but
laugh lack dey laugh in Farder Noey's time; hit
kim dough, an' de mos' uv us did n' hab no ark.

Well, ole Marse were one er dem dat did n'
t'ink war were comin'. He say hit were 'posterous
ter cornsider.

Old Miss git up what dey calls de Cabillear
blood, de blood dey nebber whup an' de blood dat

nebber holler, an' she say, " In course dey be no war. In course dey gib in ter de Rights er de States; dey gotter do hit, 'ca'se hit 's right, an' Gord on de side er de right, an' He gwine pervail 'gin de swords er de onrighteous."

But young Marse he t'ink diffunt, an' he kim home fum college widout de leabe er he Paw. Hit make ole Marse plum mad, an' he swar' he sen' him back, an' he r'ar' an' charge 'roun' ginnerly.

Ole Marse he were er Ole Line Whig, er sumpen, an' he say dat we all one country, dat gemmen settle 'litical p'ints in er 'litical way; dat Jeff Davis an' dem silber talkin' fellers on bofe sides gwine fix hit; dat only pussonel honor am settled wid de drawin' er swords an' de spillin' er blood.

But young Marse he were he own marster now, an' dey 'sult in de drawin'-room an' argufy at de table, twel hit make ever't'ing plum oncomferble.

Bimeby, dough, ole Marse sorter gib in, 'ca'se he say fur de honor er ole Massysip dat he hatter go wid his State, whichebber way she go, an' *she go out.*

My! de carryin'-on dem young folkes hab, wid de formin' er de comp'nies, an' de sewin' er de flags an' de makin' er de gray coats. De man tailors cain't sew fas' ernough, so de 'omans, dat ain't nebber did

nuffin' in dey lives try dey han's, an' Miss Jinny
were plum up wid any uv 'em. She all 'cited lack,
an' trimble an' say: "Mammy dis, an' Mammy dat,"
lack she uster when she were leetle.

How my Baby watch fur Marse Phil ter come
fum college, an' how glad she were when he kim!

Marse Phil, he sorter quiet lack, an' ain't lack de
odders; but de Baby she so yearnes' she don' see hit,
an' she say she make him de gray coat herse'f fur
him ter go out in,—my Baby, dat nebber eben hem
er pocket hankercher!

Well, dey hol' all dey meetin's an' goodbyin's in
ole Miss's drawin'-room, an' ole Marse he stomp
roun' wid de bes' uv 'em, an' gib so many hosses an'
'quip so many comp'nies, dat we all feared he bruk
hese'f.

Miss Jinny wa'n't no flirt, but ter some uv 'em she
gib her blessin', an' ter odders uv 'em she gib er
piece er de putty brown curls, fur she want 'em ter
go out fur dey principuls, an' ef dey ain't fight for
dem, ter fight fur *her*, 'ca'se de cause hern, an' she
say so.

Dey all looks mighty scrumptious at Marse Phil
when dey leabe him behin', fur Marse Phil ain't go
out yit, dough de gray coat done been done time

out'n reason. He set in de drawin'-room twel ole Marse done git plum out'n patience; an' walk an' talk wid Miss Jinny unner de live-oaks.

She mighty oneasy in her min' 'bout him, an' sometime she look mighty pitiful at him out'n dem big sof' eyes. She ain't say nuffin' yit, not eben ter her Mammy, 'ca'se she dat proud, 'ca'se she got de Cabillear blood. But in de middle er de night, I hears her moan an' cry sof' ter herse'f,—I allus sleeps in de Baby's room ebber sence she were borned. Den I calls ter her, an' I say, "What de matter, honey?" an' she say so sof', "I des been er-dreamin'; go ter sleep, Mammy."

One day ole Marse git mad an' cuss an' say 'sumpen 'bout "cowards"; de Baby git up quick an' leabe de table, but I ain't foller, 'ca'se I know sumpen hu'tin' uv her heart, dat she don' wanter tell eben ter her Mammy.

De boys writ ter us, an' we all powerful proud, an' ole Miss hol' her head higher'n ebber. Ole Miss all head an' no heart; mus' er los' dat heart somers an' ain't fin' hit no mo', so she cain't tell nuffin' 'bout de Baby.

I knows dat trouble kimmin' ter her, an' I prays 'bout hit all unbeknownst; an' hit kim all uv er heap.

I was er-settin' 'hine de sweet shrub at de aige er
de big porch, er-knittin' erway fur dear life, when
Marse Phil an' de Baby kim walkin' slow lack out
on de porch.   I did n' 'low ter stay, but I could n'
git out, 'douten dey sees me, an' hit 'pear lack dey go
in ever' minute, so I des sot an' wait.

Marse Phil's face des es white es er sheet, an' his
eyes des es hard an' brack.   I cain't see de Baby's
face fur he stan' facin' uv her, an' he measure his
words slow an' keerful, an' he says, " Furginia," says
he, " you has been er-waitin' an' er-wantin' fur me ter
go out fur er long time; you has worked fur hit, an'
has pricked your putty fingers fur hit, but I has
waited — why, you is soon gwine fur ter know.
Now I 'se gwine out."   He stop, an' I know by de
way de Baby set back dat leetle head er hern dat
she proud an' she glad.

Den he cl'ar he thote onct er twict, an' de Baby·
she say, " Well ? " so sof' an' sweet.

Den he voice sorter shake an' he say, " Furginia,
I lubs you better dan anyt'ing on dis yeth; I 'd die
fur you, an' I libs o'ny fur you.   All dat good in
me, all I is, an' all I hopes ter be, I owes ter you, an'
ter your lub fur me, an' I 'se gwine out, *but I cain't
go out on de side er de gray!* "

I see Miss Jinny trimble quick an' sof' lack de leabes on de Lombardy poplar, all tergedder.

Den she say, proud lack : "Phil, de time fur jestin' an' jokin' am pas', don' tease me now; I cain't b'ar hit!"

Den he say, "I ain't jokin', Furginia! Gord knows dat I 'se lack ter please you, but my principuls am all on de odder side. We differs in politics, but is one in lub, Furginia; fur er man hatter 'sert his manhood, but er 'oman hain't no call in 'litical p'ints, hit hain't bercomin' ter her!"

I see Miss Jinny ketch at de roses in her belt,— she allus wear 'em,—and squiz em in her han', an' speak quick an' fas' :

"When her State hab 'clared hitse'f, when her house hab 'clared hitse'f, when her brudder an' her kinsmen hab gone out on dat side! What does you mean, Phil?" an' de Baby breave short, lack hit hu't her.

Marse Phil's face git whiter an' whiter, but he speak out cl'ar an' steddy. "I means, my darlin', dat you is mine, dat I won't gib you up, not fur country, not fur State, not fur de grandes' name dat ebber crown de grandes' man, but I cain't go out on de side er de gray!"

Dey looks one nudder in de face lack dey tryin'
ter read what was writ on de odder's soul. Den I
hears er soun' an' I looks out, fur I t'inks er pattridge
feel er bullet in her heart, an' gib er cry fur de leetle
ones, but I ain't see no smoke. 'Pear lack er white
dove fum de cote, wid blood on her breas', done gib
de def-cry, but dar wa'n't no dove dar. Lord Gord!
hit were my Baby, hit were her heart!

But dat Cabillear blood gwine tell, an' she straighten
herse'f up proud lack, my po' Baby, an' she say,
"Phil, does you mean what you has said?" an' he
say slow an' solemn, lack 't were in church, "As
Gord am my witness, I does!"

Hit min' me ever' word lack de pins dey sticks in
fur ter hol' de wings uv er big, bright butterfly, an'
I sees hit flutter an' flutter, so pitiful lack, but dey
goes on stickin' de pins. I wanter say sumpen, I wants
ter tell 'em,— dey's er-breakin' er dey hearts lack dey
was saucers an' teacups 'ca'se dar were war in de lan'
an' dey differ, but I wa'n't nuffin' but er po' ole nigger
ef I were de mudder, an' I des sot an' cry. I mought
er done hit, I mought er done hit, an' hit pester
me mightily sometimes, but hit too late now.

I sees de Baby fol' her arms, I sees de blood er de
Maw in her, an' I hears it des es cole es ice.

"Den, Misser Le Grand, all bertwix' us am at er eend! Go swell de ranks es er traitor to your Souf- lan'; go spill de blood dat oughter been your pride. *What my house is, I is. Go!*"

She sweep by, two er free steps, den she mos' fall into er big cheer settin' dar. De sun were down an' hit gittin' dusky, but I see she look lack stone.

"Furginia, Furginia!" Hit seem lack Marse Phil's heart were breakin'. "Lis'en ter me. I is fixed in my b'leef er de right an' de truf, an' I 'se boun' ter 'bide by hit. What am er man widout honor? An' my honor hit say 'Go!' but oh, my lub, how can I gib you up! Furginia, gib me, grant me des your lub an' let me be er man!" He were res'in' on one knee, an' all de dark French blood were er-pleadin' fur him. I see de Baby settin' stiff an' still lack she were dead, an' she say:

"Misser Le Grand, your honor an' mine is two diffe'nt t'ings, an' bofe uv 'em cain't be right!"

He t'ink she weakenin' an' ketch he breaf an' move up closter. "Bofe b'leeve dey right, an' on'y time can prove hit," he say so eager an' yearnes' lack.

"You mistake me, Misser Le Grand," say de Baby, "an' what I b'leeves I 'se willin' ter die fur!"

Den Marse Phil git down on bofe knees. He were

er proud man, Marse Phil were. I nebber 'spec' ter lib ter see dat day; an' he say lack he talkin' ter er leetle chile, "My darlin', you is actin' uv er part, you is er-hidin' er your true, yearnes' heart; hit er bleedin', po' tender heart, but er lub lack yourn ain't gwine die, cain't die, lack dis!

"My sweetheart, my own leetle one," he cry, "say dat when all am settled, when de war done ober, dat I kin come ter Brokenburne ter claim my leetle wife!"

I hears de Baby smudder er groan; I cain't see 'em fur de dark, now. "Philip Le Grand," she say, "don' desecate dat word. Ter me hit now am sadder an' holier dan all de odders, an' fore Gord dat make me, I say dat ef you goes out on de Union side I kin nebber be your wife,—nebber, nebber!"

Dey ain't speak fur er minute. Den I hears Marse Phil say lack he chokin', "Den, Furginia, am all at er eend bertween us?"

I hears de Baby whisper, "All!"

He say, "Fur all time?" and she say lack hit were er cuss, er cuss on his life an' hern, "Maybe fur Etarnity!"

I hears Marse Phil fling sumpen on de porch an' grine hit hard an' quick wid his heel. Hit were de

pictur' dat de Baby kiss an' lub, dat she w'ar roun'
her nake!

But Marse Phil don' make no sign ner say no
word, but des turn, wid his long swingin' step,
down de walk an' inter de darkness, des lack nuffin'
happin.

We hab er turrible time dat night, me an' de
Baby, all unbeknownst, 'ca'se her ain't eben tole her
ole Mammy yet, but she lay her putty brown head
'gin dis ole brack breas', lack she uster when she were
leetle, an' cry an' cry an' say she sick an' wanter die,
—ain't nuffin' lack de stiff Cabillear lady dat telled
Marse Phil ter "Go!" But I cry wid her, too, 'ca'se
I allus cry when she cry. She stay in bed an' I fotch
her breakfus an' tell 'em she got de headache; den I
fotch her dinner an' tell 'em she got de headache, an'
hit go on dat way fur two er free days, an' nobody
ain't say nuffin' 'bout Marse Phil, 'ca'se I lis'ens
'roun' powerful fur de sakes er de Baby. 'Twel one
day she git up late in de ebenin' lookin' es white es
marvel, an' flings her pink dressin'-gown on an' goes
ter de winder an' stan's dar 'hine de curtains so 's
nobody ain't see her. I sees de Le Grand kerridge
er-comin' down de road, an' I ketches de shinin' er

3

big brass buttons in de sunlight on a blue Yankee
coat, but I ain't say nuffin'. Dey hatter pass we-all's
house on de road ter de station, hain't no gittin' roun'
hit, but I says ter myse'f, says I, "Marse Phil hain't
no sneak ef he do be gwine jine de Yanks; des putten
on he blue close an' start wid 'em right here, an' he
know dey all plum bitter ergin him now. Mought
er sneakted ter de Norf in his black coat, lack many
onnudder one done," but I lay low 'bout hit.

De Baby git whiter an' whiter an' hol' her han's so
tight, twel de rings on de leetle fingers cuttin' plum
inter de flesh. Den she say, "Mammy, Mammy,
look! come see! De traitor ter his Maker, his kentry an' ter me!"

She look one mo' time, but hit 'pear lack de sperrit uv her youf, an' de sunlight uv her joy, go out
in dat look, an' she fling herse'f on de bed an' cry,
"Oh! my Gord!" she cry, "Lemme die,—I hain't
fitten ter lib,—I hain't fitten ter look happy people
in de face no mo'!"

Hit were de blood er de farder an' de mudder
stribin' in her, de head an' de heart, an' hit 'pear lack
de soul gwine fly erway lack er white butterfly in de
stribin'. Hit make me cry now, young Marse,
dough I 'se ole an' I 'se hard, an' I 'se been frough er

heap sence den. My putty angil, my po' Baby!
'ca'se she were des lack mine. I nussed two babies,
ole Miss's an' mine, but de Lord tuck de strong
brack one, an' lef' de leetle tender white one. Look
at dis pictur', young Marse. Hit were painted 'cross
de warter somers; de Baby guv hit ter me when she
tuck hit fum Marse Phil, but es white an' es grand es
Furginia Balfour be, hit were ole brack nigger milk
make her dat way.

Well, leetle by leetle, de Baby tell me, an' I 'suade
her ter talk, fur hit do her good, but I hain't got ter
say er word 'gin Marse Phil, no my Lord! fur she
des flare up lack powder.

She keep her room whilst de whole kentry des er-
waggin' 'bout Phil Le Grand er-jinin' de Yanks.
Ole Marse he swar' an' ole Miss she plum shock'.
She high an' mighty, she des shock'; an' she say proud
lack ter de comp'ny dat come, " Dat hit were berry
unfortnit an' pervokin', 'bout de mixin' up er de
names; dat dar hain't nebber been anyt'ing ertween
Furginia Balfour an' Misser Le Grand." Po' ole
Miss! she ain't ebber ast de Baby, an' po' Baby!
she ain't nebber tell her.

Young Marse, hearts is cu'i's t'ings, boun' ter no one
er turr, but you nebber kin tell whedder dey gwine

ben' er break, twel dey done gone an' done hit, an' dat were de way wid de Baby.

Doctor kim an' say she read too much; nudder kim an' say she t'ink too much; nudder kim an' say she don' read 'nough, dat she dwellin' on sumpen.

Den, bress your soul, de Maw's spirit in her r'ar', an' she git mad an' git out'n dat bed in er jiffy an' inter de garden, but she were mighty weak an' white when de mad lef' her.

She git betterer bimeby, an' go out an' hunt up all de po' mizerbul niggers on de plantation, des ter make 'em happy,—an' my!—de t'ings de Baby guv dem ole mizerbul niggers!

Well, arter while, young Marse he kim home wid fixin's on he shoulder, an' we all dat proud er de fixin's we could n' honor him ernough. Den him an' Miss Jinny hab er long talk, an' I see 'em comin' in, he er-lookin' down, so proud an' han'some, an' her er-lookin' up wid her han' on he arm, so lovin' an' so trus'ful,— dar were er mighty strong tie ertwix' dem two, allus.

An', Lord! how high ole Miss step es she guv her orders. You t'ink she fixin' ter 'tain de Prince er Wales, an' hit were "my son dis, an' my son dat," twell we could n' res'.

'Bout dat time we heared dat Marse Phil done

kim home too; hit were sorter whispered roun', fur dar wa'n't many er dem sort in our parts. Den him an' young Marse meet an' pass one nurr in de big road 'douten de techin' er dey hats,— dem dat hab been chillun an' luvyers tergerr!

Bimeby young Marse jine he reg'mint, an' we heared as how Marse Phil done gone too,— when one night 'bout dark, some one fotch er message an' say dey some one wanter see Bene down by the orchard gate. I t'ink hit mighty quare, but howsomeebber es dey sont fur me, I goes.

I gits nigh de gate an' I sees er tall figger stan'in' dar in de shadder. Bene were mighty skeered hit were er Yank done come ter steal her, but she done make up her min' dat she ain't gwine go, when de figger hit say:

"Mam Bene, hit were me sont fur you,"—an' bress goodness! ef hit wa'n't Marse Phil!

I wa'n't nuffin' but er nigger, an' I don' know what 's 'spected uv me, I dun know wher' ter be glad er sorry, so I des fol' my arms, an' say nuffin', lack ole Miss do.

"Mam Bene," he say, " I 'se in er herry,—dey all t'ink I gone, but I could n' go 'dout seeing you. Tell me, fur Gord's sake, how she be?" His voice

3*

shake an' trimble, an' I guv in, 'ca'se I knows he lubs her yit.

Es I tells him mo' an' mo', he say, "Po' leetle girl, brave leetle heart," ober an' ober, an' drawed his sleeve 'cross his furrud lack hit were hot.

He sorter choke when I tells him how she won't let nobody 'buse him, an' arter while he say, "My time 's up."

Den he say, sof' 's er 'oman, "Mam Bene, take keer er my leetle girl. Gord only know how I lub her! I hain't no call ter glory ef I be brave. I 'd be er coward an' skulk fur her sake ef I could, but I cain't, I cain't. My manhood won't let me, an' ef hit did, she 'd hate me!"

"Mam Bene," he cry ergin, "she 's mine, she 's mine! Don' let anyt'ing happen ter her. Guard her wid your life. Take keer uv her twel she 'll let me come an' claim her, fur dat will *mus'* gib in ter mine!"

"Mam Bene," he say, eager lack, "dar mighty hard times er-comin' 'fore dis ober, times er sorrer an' suff'rin', an' dyin', an' we may n't see one nurr twel hit all cl'ar erway. Take dis,"—an' he shove sumpen hard, dat feel lack money, inter my han's. "Keep hit hid twel de hard times kim, an' don' let her want fur anyt'ing dat she been uster, not ef money kin buy hit. Hit am gole an' hit 'll pass anywhar. What-ebber you does, don' let Furginia know you seen me; ef she 'spec' de money, say de young Marse sont hit. Ef you go fum here, leabe word wid Mammy Dink at my house, an' this paper 'll pass you anywhar 'long de Fedrul lines."

Den he squiz my han' an' say, " Take keer er my leetle gal,—Gord bress you all,— goodbye!"—an' he were gone. Gone ter jine his Yanks, an' he got my Baby's heart, an' she got his'n,— my Lord!

Dun know how hit were, young Marse, but arter while hit 'pear lack we was cut off, sorter out 'n line er sumpen. Hit nebber seem fur fum folkes in time er peace. Dar was allus comin' an' gwine den, but now hit 'pear lack we way ter nowhar, an' de news we gits so stale hit no news ertall.

Miss Jinny she taken powerful ter de leetle Cat-'lick Church. Marse Phil he were er Cat'lick, but de Baby wa'n't nuffin'. Her Maw taken on powerful fur er while, but hit don' do no good, fur de Baby keep er-gwine.

We ain't got de t'ings we uster hab, but we 's got de style, fur ole Miss steps higher yit, 'counter young Marse. She set lack er queen, dough de chiny see t'ings hit nebber see erfore, an' de silber urn make de 'quaintance wid 'tater coffee.

We ain't heared fum young Marse fur er time an' we 's all mighty oneasy in de min', but we ain't say much, 'ca'se we 's all er powerful proud, secretin' fambly, but we 's cryin' an' worryin' des de same.

All uv er suddent here kim er batch er papers an' letters frough de lines. Dey was ole, but dey fotch news ernough ter we-all. Dey guv 'em ter ole Miss an' Miss Jinny, 'ca'se ole Marse cain't see 'dout his specs; an' we-all house niggers waits ter hear de news.

"'Motions," read ole Miss, sorter smilin'. "Won'erful charge,—'moted on de fiel',— *Colonel* Balfour,— hear dat?" Ole Miss do look so proud, ole Marse slap he knee an' holler, "By Jove, I knowed he would!" an' de Baby jump an' hug her Paw,—dey was allus tergedder, dese two, in joy er in sorrer. Ole Miss lub ter be proud by herse'f.

Den she open ernurr paper. Dar er long list er woun'ed an' dead fur de battle er sumpen ruther, whar de Yanks whup us plum out; I done furgit de name.

Ole Miss rin her eye down de line lack er streck, an' we hol' our breaf ter hear her say hit all right, but she nebber say hit. Po' ole Miss! so proud an' so

grand! She des straighten back stiff widout er word, wid one long white finger p'intin' at 'er name in de list er de dead.

Miss Jinny say hit were, " Colonel Balfour, de braves' orfficer er de day, is 'ported dead, but dar am no cert'ny in de 'port."

But ole Miss nebber see dat line; she des see der name uv her boy. De doctor he say it 'plexy; dat de heart been t'reatenin' fur er long time, but ole Miss ain't tell us, 'ca'se she proud; dat de shock done fetch hit on sooner dan he 'spected, and she cain't git well.

Po' ole Marse! 'pear lack he done furgit how hard an' cole she growed ter be, an' he t'ink on her lack her were young an' lovin' ergin, an' set an' smoove her long white han' lack he were in er daze, an' de Baby set at his feet an' cry, but ole Miss ain't move an' dun know nuffin' yit.

Bimeby de hard, proud look des fade erway, an' de face look des es sweet an' ca'm es er leetle chile. Ole Miss were er putty 'oman, all de grand look done gone, 'ca'se she were gittin' ready fur de Kingdom. Ole Marse nebber move one peg, but set sider de bed an' say sof' t'ings ter her, dough she cain't nebber hear 'em, an' de big tears rin down his cheeks.

Hit feel mighty quare not ter see ole Miss lookin' arter t'ings, but t'ings goes on des lack she were
dar, 'ca'se we mos' feels lack we hears her voice, an'
we prays we mought, but hit wa'n't no use. So we
sont fur her preacher an' he pray, dough ole Miss
cain't hear him. But es we stan' dar, we know she
done make her peace, fur she fetch one long, easy
breaf, er-smilin' lack she hear sumpen we ain't hear,
den go ter sleep lack er baby in de mudder's arms.
Well, we buries ole Miss an' watch de sun go down
on de new grabe,—de fus' yeth bruk fur er Balfour
in many an' many er year. Oh, hit were pitiful! an'
we all mourn yearnes' fur ole Miss, fur hit seem
lack on'y de good done lef' ter 'member her by,
an' de niggers min's her word an' does her way,
dough she dead an' gone, fur de fears er pesterin'
her in de grabe, an' fur de layin' uv her sperrit.

Ole Marse he 'pear ter des let go, but de Baby put
her leetle white shoulder ter de wheel an' her ole
Mammy holp her b'ar de load.

'Pear lack ole Marse sorter wander in de min' an'
he t'ink he young ergin, an' sometimes he call Miss
Jinny by de Maw's name. Po' Baby! I sees her
turn her head an' her lip trimble when she answer,
but she des fotch him back lack he were er leetle

chile. Den ole Marse git ter talkin' 'bout Marse
Phil an' r'ar' an' charge lack he uster, on'y he weaker,
an' say Miss Jinny done fixin' ter leabe him, ter rin
erway wid Marse Phil; dat she were false an' ontrue
wid de fust traitor blood dat ebber warm de heart uv
er Balfour; ter go 'long wid her Yank, dat right;
ter leabe her ole farder ter die fur he principuls.
She git white an' shake, lack she hab de agur, an'
her voice trimble, but she soove him an' soove him
twel he t'ink he talkin' ter de Maw 'bout de two
leetle chillun, an' he laugh sorter low, an' 'low dat
" Mammy spilin' dat gal sho." Well, t'ings w'ar on
so po'ly, what wid worryin' an weepin', de Baby git
so white an' thin dat I 'se 'feared de angils kim in de
night-time an' take her 'way all unbeknownst, an' I
gits up ter ease my min' an' feels in de bed ef she
dar; she dar, an' she gits up in de mornin' an' go
frough de same ole t'ing.

We 'se all 'feared young Marse kilt sho' 'nough,
'ca'se we hain't heared nuffin' sense de paper whar ole
Miss read. Then one dark day when hit 'pear
lack ole Marse wan'erin' worser an' worser, an' hit
'pear lack de Baby could n' libe frough hit no longer,
er foot scrunch on de grabble in de walk, er man
wid his arm in er sling step up on de porch, an'

Miss Jinny, lack er bird dat done foun' er res' at las', wid er leetle sof' cry, fol' young Marse in her arms!

'Pear lack young Marse wa'n't dead arter all.   He were woun'ed an' los' he head fum de flowin' er de blood, an' dey lef' him on de fiel' fur dead.

Bimeby, when hit git dark, he kim to, an' some one hear him groan an' make er light; he dun know who he were, an' de man retch in young Marse's pockets ter fin' out who he be, an' pull out er pictur' er de Baby (de mate ter dis one here, young Marse) an' when he strike ernurr light an' look, he say: "My Gord! my Gord!" but young Marse too weak ter see who hit were yit.   Den de man lay de pictur' sof' lack in de pocket ergin.

Bimeby, young Marse fin' hese'f in er horsepittle, wid er lot er woun'ed Yankees, an' he stay dar fur mont's an' mont's, not knowin' er keerin'.   'Pear lack de man sont word ter ole Marse an' dem, but dey nebber git hit,— on'y de papers wid de 'port.

Young Marse ast ter see de man what sont him dar, but he ain't come, an' bimeby, when he git better, he say he gwine; when de nuss brung him er letter an' hit say: "My brudder, you dun know who sabed you, an' I t'ink hit bes' fur him not ter see you, onless hit could do some good, fur he who

sabed you am er brudder, not er foe. Dese here
dun know who you be, an' you hain't no cause ter
tell 'em. I tuck your gray close 'fore I fotch you
here. You kin fin' 'em whar I tells you. I sont
your people word. Go home fur her sake. Don't
enter de sarvice ergin twel you git well. Now you
know who I is."

Dar were money too in de letter fur ter fotch
young Marse home dat Marse Phil ain't say anyt'ing
erbout. Young Marse writ er letter an' t'ank him;
he could n' holp dat. But he sont de money back,
'ca'se unner de sarcumstances he 'ferred ter foot hit
all de way home.

Young Marse hear 'bout he Maw bein' dead 'fore
he git here, an' what kilt her, an' hit go mighty hard
wid him, wid dat deep hu'tin' dat las'es so long.

Hit take young Marse's arm er power er time ter
git well, an' arter er while we a'mos' git cheerful lack;
ole Marse bein' sometimes worser an' sometimes
betterer in he min', an' we all humors him powerful.

He still r'ar' 'bout Marse Phil an' Miss Jinny; he
cain't unnerstan' 'bout he sabin' er young Marse, so
he an' Miss Jinny hain't call de name bertwix' 'em
sence he telled 'em.

Bimeby young Marse's arm git well, his duty call

him, an' he hatter go. He look er long time at Miss
Jinny, wid her eyes so big an' dark an' her face so
white; he look er long time at he Paw, broken,
bented, settin' in de big cheer, talkin' lack er leetle
chile sometimes, but he hatter go.

He bury he head in he han's, den raise he face,
white an' drawed wid pain, an' say, "Take keer uv
'em, Mammy!"

So young Marse go down de big walk, an' all de
sunlight go down wid him fur me an' de Baby.

Arter dat t'ings goes on slow lack an' out'n gear.
Ole Marse he fail day arter day, lack de sun goin'
down slow but sho', an' Miss Jinny she griebe an'
griebe.

I t'inks 'bout de money Marse Phil guv me, but
we got 'nough ter eat, an' money cain't buy helf
an' happiness, dough she uster bofe, so I keeps hit
hid.

Some days Miss Jinny git mighty low, an' go
'bout wid de putty brown eyes red and swelled lack
all day. I knows what hit were, 'ca'se I 'se er 'oman.
I castes 'bout what ter say. Den I says, desprit lack,
says I ('ca'se I knows she kin tell her sumpen),
"Honey, 'sposin' I sen' Aaron arter Mammy Dink
ter come holp me, 'ca'se I got er mizry." She sorter

kin ter Aaron, an' uster come sometimes 'fore we all taken sides.

Den de Baby raise dem long heaby lashes an' say, " No, you hain't, Mammy; hit me got de mizry." Den she say rale low, " No, you cain't, Mammy."

Den I say, " Don't you lub him no mo', honey?" She raise her eyes solemn lack, an' say, " Yas, Mammy, I do lub him!"

Den I say, " What you breakin' your heart fur, Baby; 'ca'se folks wanter fight an' die, is you gotter die too?"

She shake her head so sad lack, an' say, "Mammy, 'dout meanin' any disrespec' ter you, 'ca'se I lubs you, you is er nigger, Mammy, an' er slabe; you cain't unnerstan' de free-born blood, de blood dat 'll die by de cause, an' be glad er de chances. Hit de principuls, Mammy, hit de principuls, and I 'se 'feared I 'se er weak 'oman. I 'd lay down my life an' die fur 'em, but oh, my Gord! hit 's de libin' widout him! But he mus' nebber, nebber know hit, Mammy; he mus' t'ink dat my lub am dead, dat I 'se true ter my house, an' I will be true, Mammy!"

'T 'ain't no use ter argufy, an' I ain't. She speak de Gord's truf: I cain't unnerstan'!

Ole Marse done fail an' fail now, twel ever'body

see es how he cain't las' much longer,—all 'cep'in' Miss
Jinny, an' she keep er-hopin' 'gin hope, 'ca'se she say
de Lord hain't gwine take 'em all fum her. He
gwine leabe one. But he hain't gwine leabe ole
Marse. He were one kine er dem folkes, honey, dat
de Lord make er call fur him ter ben', an' he cain't
do hit, he des hatter break. We tries ter git word
ter young Marse, but we cain't; we writes an'
writes, an' we ain't hear nuffin'. Ole Marse see how
hit were, an' he tries so hard ter lib,—po' ole Marse!
He nebber wanter gib no trouble ef he kin holp it,
but he des could n' make er stan' 'gin' def, dat kim
er-creepin' an' er-creepin' in de daylight an' de
darkness.

De Baby she fix him an' prop him in his big cheer,
an' comb he ha'r an' tell him how putty he look, an'
sing ter him, an' make jokes fur him ter laugh, wid
her po' heart des er-breakin' all de time, an' all de
time de call des er-knockin' at de do'.

Honey, we 's all gotter hear dat call; hain't no beg-
gar's rags gwine hide him, an' hain't no king's do'
dat 'll shet hit out. Hain't no lub gwine make hit
wait, an' hain't no hate gwine herry hit. Hit kim
ter all do's an' hit kim ter ourn. Sometime 'fore
hit kim de min' dat wan'erin' all kim back, des

es ca'm an' strong, an' hit were dat way wid ole Marse.

De Baby feel so happy 'bout hit an' hum er leetle song ter herse'f; she allus do dat way when she happy, an' I hain't let on, 'ca'se hit break dis ole heart fur ter spile one minute fur her. He talk ter me private lack, when she ain't dar, an' make all de 'rangements quiet lack.

At las' dar were er great change, eben de Baby t'ink he lookin' po'ly an' bad, an' he call de Baby ter him, an' tell me ter wait dar, lookin' mighty yearnes', an' I waits,—'pear lack ever't'ing waitin',— an' he say, "Furginia," says he, "my chile, I hain't got long ter stay, an' I got some t'ings ter tell you dat I done putten off long 'nough. You has been er comfort an' er joy ter me ebber sence I knowed er leetle gal chile were borned ter me, an' I t'ank Gord fur sen'in' you, ever' day dat I lib, but now I feels I got ter go, an' gwine be wid your mudder 'fore long."

De Baby could n' say nuffin', but des stan' dar, wid de big tears er-drappin' off'n her lashes lack rain, an' ole Marse smoove an' pat de leetle white han' while he talk.

"I done make my 'rangements ter go, all unbe-

4

knownst ter you, 'ca'se I did n' wanter burden you
'fore de time—hit were fur de bes'.   Don' cry, my
darter, fur you hu't me, hu't me so I cain't talk."
Ole Marse still look at de leetle han' an' pat hit sof'
ergin.   "You is mighty leetle an' Mammy mighty
ole ter leabe here all erlone, but I cain't wait, an' you
hatter do de bestes' you kin twel de Colonel kim
home."   (We allus gib young Marse his 'titlement
when we names him, an' ole Marse ain't furgit.)
"When my boy come home, tell him he make his
farder proud 'fore he died."

He still hol'in' de Baby's han', an' 'pear lack he
countin' de leetle fingers.   I 'low ter sen' Aaron fur
de doctor, but ole Marse he say stern lack, "I 'se
heared de call, Mammy, an' I 'se ready ter go; I wants
my las' hour ter be er hour er peace."

I 'low ter sen' Aaron fur de preacher, but ole Marse
'low he don' want him.   He say, "I done make my
peace long ergo; hit er mighty po' Christian, Mammy,
dat 'll wait fur def ter skeer 'im inter salvation."

Ole Marse know what he want.   He des er-talkin'
right erlong now lack hese'f, so we all des wait.

De Baby 'pear lack she unner er spell er sumpen.
I hain't nebber see her eyes so big er her face so
white, an' she des look at ole Marse lack she tryin'

ter charm his soul wid hern frough her eyes. Ole
Marse say lack 't were in er dream:

" I hain't got long ter wait. I 'se goin' out wid de
tide, an' she rinnin' out fas'."

Den he riz on he elbow an' look de Baby squar' in
de face. She were kneelin' by de bed an' trimblin'
lack er leaf. Den he say, " Furginia, de Balfours
kim f'um er long line er brave men an' noble 'omen,
an' dey hain't any uv 'em ebber shame de name;
what dey b'leeve dey libs by, an' dey died by. I
hain't 'feared er de boy, an' I hain't 'feared er you,
my darter, but Gord make er 'oman cu'i's,—hatter
make her dat way fur de sabin uv her soul. I hain't
layin' any lines on you, my darter, but I want you
ter holp me die happy."

I knowed what were comin' an' hit gwine fall
mighty heaby, an' I prays fur ole Marse ter change
he min' 'fore he speak out, but hit boun' ter come.
Den I prays quick an' fas' dat Miss Jinny mought
argufy de case des er leetle, but she were true ter
de principuls an' true ter de blood. She git whiter
an' whiter, but she wait.

De tide were mos' rin out,—de nigh bars looks
high an' dry frough de openin' in de oaks; an' ole
Marse lay wid his eyes shet lack he sleepin'.

De tide still rinnin'; de far bars shows er leetle rim. Den suddent lack ole Marse springs right up in de bed an' he whispers, " I 'se goin'! I 'se mos' gone! Promise me, promise, 'fore hit too late!" He look wild lack an' hol' Miss Jinny's arm lack he cain't let her go. She open her mouf fur de fust time an' say sumpen, but hit soun' lack hit were 'way off, an' I cain't hear fur de ringin' in my ears. Den ole Marse, wid his face all drawed, raise his voice loud an' cl'ar, " Promise, promise me, no matter which erway de war may turn, no matter who am false er who am true, dat your farder's blood shall nebber cross wid de blood uv er Le Grand!"

De Baby ain't move. She git whiter an' whiter, an' lif' her eyes lack she talkin' ter Gord. De fingers on her arm git tighter an' tighter; 'pear lack dey gwine mash de bone.

Den ole Marse glar' roun' wid he face all workin' lack he sees sumpen ebil, an' he say, " Promise, promise quick!"

She drap dem eyes dat been er-'munin' wid her Maker,—she strong 'nough now, fur He done comfort her,—an' she look ole Marse squar' in de eyes, dat glassin' now, an' gittin' dim, an' she say loud an' cl'ar, fearin' he moughten hear her, " Farder, I promise!"

l dun know how hit were den, but she were down on her knees, de farder's han' were res'in' on de curls, an' de smile dat lay roun' ole Marse's face were mixin' up de joy er Heaben wid de tears er de yeth.

I let 'em be. De tide were all rin out,— I sot an' wait; de darkness crope an' crope, an' lack de ole worl' were er great big nes', de black wing kiver all.

Young Marse, de jedgment hain't gwine ter fetch no solemner time ter me dan de day arter ole Marse die. De Baby hain't cry yit, but go 'bout busy an' white, wid her eyes des es dry an' er-shinin' lack two stars. She do all de orderin' an' 'rangin' lack she were er man. We hain't heared fum young Marse an' she taken de son's place. Dar wa'n't many ter 'ten' de funul, on'y de nighes' frien's, fur de Baby want hit quiet. Wid me an' her es de mourners, we lays him sider ole Miss an' leabes 'em tergedder in de starlight. De Baby 'fuse ter go home wid any er dey frien's, er ter let 'em stay wid her; she gwine stay home an' her ole Mammy gwine stay wid her.

She set down ter tea all erlone an' de shadders fall heaby an' heaby. Er whup'will call fum out de woods, de pine-trees moans, an' de tide sob wid hit, but hit 'pear lack de Baby cain't cry. I 'se feared

4*

fur her min', fur 't ain't in de natur' uv er 'oman ter
do dat way.   I talks 'bout de time when her an' de
brudder was leetle, an' how proud ole Marse an' ole
Miss was, an' how de leetle feet keep ole Mammy so
busy, an' how we-all went trabblin' in de summer, an'
how ever'body des take ter ole Marse fur de good
dat in him.   How arter while, he keep de school
'ports, so proud lack, in he desk, an' he w'ar de leetle
"honor medals" on he watch-guard, an' he brag on he
boy an' he brag on he gal, twel ever'body hatter jine
in; an' how he gib er breakdown ter all de niggers
ever' year when de chillun kim fum school.

De Baby ain't blink dem eyes yit, dough I knows
she lis'enin'.   Den I say, "Honey, you hab de bestes'
Paw er gal ebber hab; don' you know hit, Baby?"
Her lip sorter trimble, an' she shiver lack she callin'
her soul back fum de grabe.   Den I say, "Hain't
you sorry he gone, honey?—dat you hain't hear him
call on dis yeth no mo',—de bestes' farder an' de
bestes' Marster was ebber make fur er nigger errer
chile!"

She shiver all ober ergin, den make one soun' an'
fling herse'f in dese ole arms.   De storm hab come,
an' she cry hard lack her heart done broke.   I t'ank
de good Lord, fur I knows her min' done safe now,

an' I lets her cry an' cry an' soove her lack I 'se
done many er time erfore.

Well, t'ings goes on mighty lack dey do erfore,
'ca'se dey all knows de ways, an' ef dey 'pear ter furgit 'em, me an' Aaron des jog 'em er leetle. What
dem niggers know 'bout freedom? Um! what dey
know 'bout slabery yit? Dey got dey cabin an' dey
pig, dey got 'nough ter eat,—dey happy,—'ca'se hit
more 'n heap er quality white folks git den.

De roses kim wid de butterflies an' de autumn
kim wid its red leabes, but we hain't hear fum
young Marse yit. We gits papers now an' den,
an' Aaron hear 'em talkin' when he go ter de sto', an'
dat all we-all hears.

Some 'low hit all up, an' some 'low hit hain't, an'
dat how it stan', dough we lis'ens wid bofe years
open.

De Baby res'less lack in de house an' spen' mos'
her time in de grabeyard. I let her 'lone fur hit
holp ter make her ca'm, fur hit 'pear lack ter me,
dat de lub er Gord gwine let ole Marse's sperrit
come down fur ter comfort de sorrerin' chile.

'Bout de time I t'ink dat Miss Jinny gwine lib,
here come Mammy Dink all in er heap an' er flutter.

"Bene," she say, "we done git sech turrible news. I rid in er herry ter fotch hit!"

"Yas," I says,— "I 'se heard bad news trabble fas'. I t'ink we got trouble ernough at dis here house douten borryin'." I dun know how she stan', an' I hain't gwine 'mit myse'f fust.

"Fur de lub er Heaben, Bene!" she say, wid de big tears rinnin' down her face,— fur she were hu't, 'ca'se she were de same ter Marse Phil dat I were ter de Baby,—"don' stan' dar lack er alligater er some sech creetur, when young Marse Phil layin' at de pint er def in some sort er Yankee horsepittle, an' dey hain't no kin er his'n kin go ter comfort him!"

"My Lord!" I 'low,—"my Gord!"

I git Mammy Dink inter de kitchen 'dout makin' any mo' noise 'n I kin holp, an' I lis'ens ter de story an' castes hit 'bout in my min'. Hit were er mighty 'sponsible place ter put er po' brack nigger in, but dat nigger were de mudder an' de farder too, now, an' she gotter do erbout.

Miss Jinny don' go off de place, an' ef I hain't tell her 'bout hit she won't hear hit twel he die, ef he do die. Ef I does tell her, what good hit gwine do?— hit des make de heart bleed de mo', for hain't dat promise stan'in' lack de sword er def 'twix' her an'

young Marse Phil! Ole Marse Phil cain't go, fur
he des es holpless es er baby, an' Mammy Dink say
he des set an' cry an' cry. Ole Marse Phil hain't got
no wife, fur lo! dese many years long gone, an' de
onlies' darter were layin' low wid er leetle baby.
My po' Baby hain't got nuffin' ter hinder her, nuffin',
—nuffin' but de promise! I t'ink I talk an' 'sult wid
Aaron, but I 'members hit 's de Baby's secret, so I
prays an' wrastles an' wrastles an' prays, an' makes
Mammy Dink lay low unbeknownst.

In de long night I lays, an' I tries ter put myse'f in
de Baby's place, so 's ter do what I t'ink she want me
ter do. Bimeby, I dozes off, an' ever' time I 'clude
ter tell her in de dream, de promise riz up lack er big
brack cross an' hide de sunlight, an' de sun go down
in darkness. But she settle hit herse'f.

She kim in, in de mornin', lookin' so sad lack, in
her brack dress, wid er big white butterfly dat de
fros' done tuck short, er flutterin' an' er flutterin' on
her han', but hit cain't fly. She look at hit plum
sorrerful, an' try ter holp hit, but hit day done gone.
Dar 's er cu'i's sayin' 'mongst ole folks 'bout dem
white butterflies, young Marse, an' my min' misgibes
me. 'Pears lack I hears 'er call fum somers es she
stan' dar, wid her putty head bent down, techin' dem

po' wings, when she say suddent lack, " Mammy, has
you heared anyt'ing fum Mam Dink lately ? "

I drops de shammy dat I been polishin' de silber
wid, an' say, " Lord! Baby, why ? " Niggers is
sech cute 'ceitful creeturs, dey is, young Marse, dey
cain't holp hit. She ain't call no names, but she say,
" I knows sumpen done gone wrong wid him."

Den I ups an' tells her all I knows, an' she sen' fur
Mam Dink.

Mam Dink goes home nex' day sorter pestered
lack, an' de Baby hain't say nuffin'. But onct er
twict I hears her pleadin' an' prayin' in de middle er
de night, but I hain't no call fur ter pester her, 'ca'se
she know her Mammy true.

Bimeby Mam Dink kim back,—hit were hard ridin'
fur her ole bones, fur she were heap oler 'n me,—an'
fotch er paper she won't lay in nobody's han's but
Miss Jinny's.

I nebber knowed what hit were, 'ca'se I nebber
larned ter read, an' Miss Jinny nebber told me, but
I fin's her wid dat paper squiz up in her han', an' dat
han' were pressin' on her heart, cole an' still lack she
were dead. Mammy's po' Baby! she 'd er b'ared
hit all fur her ef she could,—she 'd er let 'em

drawed de blood outen her drap by drap, ter sabe
dat chile!

I baves her face twel hit fotch her to, an' brung de
wine fur her, an' when she drink hit, she lay de putty
brown head close up ter me, wid de eyes shet an' de
warter trimblin' on de long lashes, an' she say, whis-
perin', " Talk ter me sof', Mammy, lack I were
er leetle chile, Mammy, 'ca'se I gotter be strong
soon, Mammy."

My Baby, my leetle one, she ain't got nobody
but her po' ole Mammy ter lub her, but Gord! how
dat Mammy lub her!

When she ca'm, she go down ter de leetle wicket
gate, an' I follers, but she wave me back, an' say, " I
be back bimeby, Mammy, hit all right!" I watches
her long 's I kin see her, an' I knows she gwine ter
Farder Lucien. Miss Jinny ain't no Cat'lick, ner
none er her folks was, but Marse Phil were. Den I
waits in de grabeyard fur her; I allus meets her dar
ebery ebenin'.

She pray long an' yearnes' ober ole Marse's grabe,
an' dat night she writ an' writ mos' all night. In de
mornin' she sont fur Aaron an' shet de do', de fust
time she ebber do dat sence she were bornced. When
he kim out he drawed his sleeve ober his eyes an'

set an' sniff an' sniff in de kitchen, 'steader gwine ter work, but he ain't say nuffin'.

I bides my time, an' bimeby I picks hit out'n Aaron,—he cain't keep nuffin' fum me yit,—an' he got er ring dat Miss Jinny gib him ter git money on, someway. Po' Baby! she dun know no mo' 'bout money dan er angil! Hit were er leetle shiny ring dat uster laugh on dem leetle fingers, when we all was happy an' dem leetle fingers had er dimple on ever' leetle j'int, an' I taken hit fum Aaron an' putten hit in my pocket. Po' Baby! es pure an' white es de lilies in de New Jerusalem! What she know 'bout gittin' money on t'ings, an' who gwine buy 'em?

While she sleep, I taken Marse Phil's bag er gole an' de pass, an' lay hit by her piller. When she wake, I say: "Mammy's right foot burn,—dat mean er journey ter go, — is we gwine anywhar, Baby?"

Den she fin' de bag er gole an' break down, an' say she 'low erfore ter tell me but she cain't. She ain't ast whar de gole kim fum; maybe she t'ink Gord sont hit, fur she say, sof' lack: "Mammy, we gwine. I cain't break de promise ter my farder—we gwine, but not *Furginia Balfour!*"

I t'ink she waverin' in her min', but she tell de niggers what ter do, twel she kim back, lack er man.

I hain't no call, young Marse, ter 'spute wid sper-
rits, but dar was sumpen hol'in' her up an' 'munin'
wid her in dem days; she go right 'long an' nebber
go wrong, an' I des knows now dat hit were de
blessed Jesus er-leadin' uv her.

Well, yearly one mornin' we says "Good-by!"
ter Brokenburne; de Baby pulls her long veil ober
her face an' we was gone. Gone fum de sunlight
dat hab been, gone fum de happy times we knowed,
fur hit 'pear lack de Lord done furgit His own. But
He hain't furgit, young Marse, He hain't furgit one ob
us, 'ca'se sometimes He buil'in' de Heabenly Kingdom, an' we des er-watchin' an' honin' fur de yethly,
des lack Judas, perzackly lack Judas,—we wants ter
gib de Marster er call ter do hit, po' worfless humin
creeturs! Cain't see no furder dan Prince dar, an' he
stone blin'.

Well, I totes de money an' ten's ter de t'ings de
bestes' I kin, 'ca'se I don' wanter bodder de Baby, an'
she looks outen de winder, an' we goes er-whirlin'
an' er-whirlin', but her heart ain't dar; hit go furder
an' fas'er dan de cars kin cairey her.

My min' misgib me, an' I steddy de words,—
"We 's gwine, Mammy, but not Furginia Balfour,"
an' I 'se feared fur her min', 'ca'se she were des lack

er piece er ole Miss's chiny, an' I des gits so I falls ter sleep er-prayin' an' I wakes wid er pra'r des er-fillin' up my mouf.

Hain't nobody gib us no trouble, dough we hatter wait er while, sometimes, on de road. Ever'body look so pitiful at my Baby wid her leetle slim figger, an' long brack veil, an' de ole nigger dat tryin' so hard fur ter take keer uv her. De Souferners des know she Soufern, an' de Yanks knows we got some claim on 'em fum de pass. Bofe on 'em ast me questings, dey want ter fin' out sumpen; but de ole Marse allus uster 'low, " When you trabbles, keep your mouf shet; ef you 'se er fool errer Sol'm'n, de worl' hain't gwine know de differns," an' I does hit.

Hit git heap col'er, an' fum de quick snappy way de new folkes on de cars talks, I knows we in er furrin lan'; leastways I hain't ebber been dar erfore.

Den in de middle er de night, de cars stops, an' we lan's in er great big strange place. I hain't know what ter do, but de Baby know, an' I trus' her.

Dey cairey us ter er big house whar dey hain't put de lights out yit, but let 'em burn all de time, an' dey burnin' dim, 'an dey shows us inter er sorter leetle parlor. Den 'pear lack de Baby git res'less lack an' could n' wait, an' lock dem leetle fingers tergerr, twel I mos' cries, er-lookin' at 'em, but she ain't say nuffin' yit. Bimeby, er Cat'lick Sister kim in, an' de Baby gib her er letter. "Ah!" she say, "Farder Lucien,"—she read on, an' den she tuck de Baby's han' in hern, an' she smile so sof' an' sad, an' she say: "You begin your work in de mornin'."

"No, now, please!" say de Baby, wid her han's fol'ed an' dem eyes raise lack she were astin' sumpen er Gord.

"As you will, den," say de Sister, an' she lead her out slow an' tender, lack she were er leetle chile.

De Baby done furgit 'bout de po' ole Mammy, an' de ole Mammy cain't unnerstan' what hit mean.

I sot an' wait, an' wait, an' bimeby, I sees de Sister comin' back. I 'se mos' erfeared, 'ca'se I by myse'f, an' I dun know nuffin' 'bout dat 'ligion; I 'se er Baptis', I is, young Marse. But dat leetle Sister kim nigh an' er nigher, 'pear lack I see dat face erfore, an' she say, "Mammy!" Hit were Miss Jinny! Hit were de Baby!

"Mammy!" she say, an' she drap on her knees an' fling her arms 'roun' her ole Mammy's nake, "I gwine be true ter de libin' an' de dead, an' dey hain't nobody ter holp me but you an' my Gord! Pray, Mammy, pray dat I be able ter b'ar hit,—

pray dat de Lord keep me in de right, dat he hain't turn fum me altogedder! Pray, pray fur your chile, Mammy!"

I hain't know how I done hit, an' I dun know nuffin' 'bout Marse Phil, an' I dun know nuffin' 'bout dat 'ligion an' dat veil, but I knowed dat heart, an' I knowed hits trouble an' hits triberlatin', an' I knowed hit were hones' in de sight er de Lord, an' I raises er pra'r an' prays wid her twel she ca'm an' her eyes shines an' she jine in an' pray fur herse'f and pray fur Marse Phil an' pray fur me, twel hit 'pear lack to me de gates er de Heabenly Kingdom des er-shinin' on de ole brack yeth.

Den she riz es white an' es ca'm es de odder Sister dat kim in ter meet her. Den she say, "Mammy, I 'se er Sister er Char'ty, I come ter nuss Philip Le Grand; I hain't come es his promise' wife, I hain't come es his frien', but I comes in de name er de Lord. Ef de Lord see fitten fur to let him know my yethly name, hit 'll be all right; ef He hain't see fitten, I leave hit in His han's."

I cain't sleep dat night fur follerin' de Baby; she des de Baby ter me, hain't no Sister er de Po' spite er de close, an I begs her lemme nuss him, 'ca'se she hain't strong. She shake her head an' wave me back, but I follers. Somehow, we 's seed so much dat ever't'ing 'pear natchel when hit kim.

She know des whar ter go, an' she lead de way inter er big room, whar dar were long rows er leetle white beds wid sodgers in 'em woun'ed, sick, suff'rin', dyin'; dey hain't Yanks no mo' ter me, des po' hu'ted boys, erway fum dey mudders.

I des knowed which were Marse Phil's, an' I stan's erpart, an' turn my back, 'ca'se I don' wanter cotch de fust look de Baby gib him. Marse Phil were mighty bad. All frough de long hours we watches by him, me an' de Baby, wid des er leetle screen ter cut us off fum de res' er de suff'rin' an' de dyin'. We see him toss an' turn wid de fever, an' call on de Baby's name, ober an' ober so pitiful an' pleadin'; de big tears drap on her tellin' beads, an' I knows she prayin'. Den she move de pillers an' wring out de clorfs fur his head des lack er angil, so sweet an' still; she won't let me tech him, an' I cain't do nuffin' but des look an' look. Marse Phil he cain't git well wid er ball in he head an' er ball in he shoulder, —Cornfedrit balls! — yit dey keeps on fightin', killin', bofe uv 'em,—keeps on breakin' hearts, crossin' lub wid bay'nets an' life wid bullets! I 'se er Cornfed, young Marse, 'ca'se my folkes was, but I dun know who were right, an' sometimes when I look t'ings in de face es dey is, I 'se mos' er-feared dat bofe was wrong.

Well, we watches by Marse Phil, day arter day, an' mos' all night, wid de leetle sister er-settin' dar, er-growin' whiter an' whiter, leetler an' leetler, an' I looks out on de snow er-fallin', an' I hears Marse Phil er-talkin' ter young Marse an' ter de leetle gal dat were his promise' wife, an' he breave longer an' ca'mer, lack he happy, an' smile an' whisper 'bout when he kim back fum college. An' I sees de roses an' de sunlight on de ole porch, — ole Marse, ole Miss, young Marse, an' Miss Jinny, all happy, no war, no sorrer, no nuffin'!

Den I sees de doctors an' de nusses comin', gwine, gwine 'douten er soun'; an' de leetle sister wid her med'cine an' her spoon, an' er po' ole nigger watchin' uv 'em. Dat ole nigger sho' were me, an' de leetle sister were my Baby, an' we fur 'way fum home, whar de sun shine; up 'mong de clouds an' de snow, in er Yankee sodgers' horsepittle. When Marse Phil do dat way, I gits ter wan'erin' myse'f, an' I dun know wher I 'se libin', er I 'se dead an' riz.

One mornin' we fin's de fever all gone; hain't no mo' turnin' an' turnin', an' Marse Phil lay wid he eyes shet, lack he dead. De doctors hain't gib no mo' med'cine. I dun know nuffin' 'bout woun's,— de woun's dat war make,—an' maybe,—hope ergin' hope,—Marse Phil gwine git well. Anyway, I ups an' astes de doctor in de passage.

"No, auntie,"—he say;—"on'y Gord kin do dat."

Dey puts mo' screens erbout, an' de day w'ar on. De sun break out frough de clouds an' shine lack gole specks on de white; de leetle cole birds kim an' sot on de winder-sill an' wait fur some one ter feed 'em, but dey done furgit 'em.

De priestes kim, an' dey do fur Marse Phil what dey 'ligion tell 'em do, dough Marse Phil ain't know nuffin' yit,—an' we all kneels down. Bimeby, dey leabe we all erlone, — me, Marse Phil, an' de leetle sister.

Bimeby Marse Phil's fingers flutters on de cover-lid lack leetle white birds dat tryin' fly erway.

De leetle sister go an' kneel by de bed ter pray.

She waitin' fur de Lord ter gib de sign; an' ef hit right, she know He gwine make hit.

Arter while, de sunlight kim er-trimblin' 'cross de bed, so bright an' putty, lack hit huntin' fur er place ter res', an' Marse Phil move an' fling his arm ober his head, an' say,—"Oh! de pity uv hit,—oh! de pity!"

De Baby look at him so yearnes', lack she po'in' out her soul des lack water. Den he open he po' sunk' eyes, an' de soul er de man look inter de soul er de 'oman.

"Furginia!" he whisper.

"Philip!" she say, an' de leetle head sink an' sink an' drap on Marse Phil's breas'.

'T ain't no use ter say no mo', fur de Lord done make His sign, an' dey all done seen hit; he, 'douten her tellin' uv him, an' she know hit too. Dat one word,—hit were de "Good-bye!" er de yeth, an' de "Howdy!" uv etarnity!

She lay him back wid de smile er Gord on de parted mouf, an' go out,—out inter de night dat comin', out inter de snow,—an' I hain't no call ter foller uv her.

Hit wa'n't my Baby dat kim back,—hit wa'n't my chile!—hit were de leetle Char'ty Sister!

Dey sen' Marse Phil's body home, an' dey bury him sider he Maw.

We ain't go, an' we lets folkes say what dey pleases.

Dey sen' de Baby home too, fur ter wait er year

'fore she take de veil fur good, so 's ter be sho' in her min'.

Soon arter we kim, Mam Dink kim wid onnudder paper, an' de Baby sont one back. But dey hain't nobody hear nuffin', 'ca'se dey hain't nobody know nuffin' but me an' Farder Lucien.

But I hain't nebber git clost ter de Baby sence de day Marse Phil die; 'pear lack sumpen des er-drawin' an' er-drawin' her erway.

De niggers lubs her yit, but dey 'se 'feared uv her now, an' ef her wa'n't de chile I nuss an' I raise, I 'd be 'feared uv her myse'f. Dough she ain't w'arin' uv 'em now, somehow I allus sees de Char'ty close, an' dey 'pear lack grabeclose ter me.

We spen's heap er times in de grabeyard, 'ca'se all we 's got dar, 'cep'in' young Marse, an' 'pear lack we cain't hear fum him. Maybe he dead, too, we says, an' den de Baby bow her head, lack ter say dat she kin b'ar anyt'ing dat gwine come now.

Bimeby, Farder Lucien come, an' go an' talk ter her, fur ter see ef she in de same min' yit. De year mos' out an' hit drawin' nigh de time fur her ter take de veil sho' nough, ef she ain't change her min'.

She smile her sof', sorrerful smile, an' say she ain't change, dat she be ready when de time kim.

6

I ain't say much. I knows dat she gwine take de
veil, but de angils gwine make dat veil, an' she gwine
w'ar hit wid er crown. Ef I wa'n't nuffin' but er po'
ole nigger, maybe I mought er holp her, maybe I
mought better her, but 'fore Gord, young Marse,
I could n', an' I dun know who mought but Gord.
Hit break my heart fur ter see her w'arin' ever' day,
shadderer an' shadderer, fur de doctor he shake he
head an' say he cain't retch hit, an' Farder Lucien he
pray fur de day er de cornsecratin'. De eend were
nigher dan dey 'spec's, an' I knowed hit.

Hit happin one night, an' I wakes fum er deep
slumbrin' ter hear her call, "Mammy! Mammy!"
onct er twict, an' I riz up quick, fur I heared
onnudder call, des es sho' es Sam'l heared de call er
de Lord, an' I lays my han' on her an' say, "Baby,
here Mammy!" I make er light an' she say,
"Mammy, you is mighty nigh ter me, you has been
ever't'ing ter me, ever sence Gord tuck de odders."
I tells her dat she allus er comfort an' er joy ter her
Mammy, ever sence she were borned, an' allus
gwine be.

She sorter smile fur erway, an' say, "Not fur long,
Mammy, not fur long!"

I wanter sen' fur Farder Lucien, fur somebody,

but she ain't want ter be pestered. She say, "All well wid me, Mammy. Guard t'ings when I gone lack you done when I here, an' meet my brudder when he come. Tell him we tried ter wait twel he come, but we could n'."

I cain't do nuffin', I cain't say nuffin', but des cry.

"Po' Phil!" she say, "Gord know which were right!"

She wait erwhile, an' den she say suddent lack, "Mammy, when I done dead, let 'em bury me sider Philip Le Grand; I 'se done kep' my promise, hit won't do any harm, an' den we bofe wake at de same time in de mornin'." I promise hit de bes' I kin.

"Mammy," she say, "ef dey looks in my heart, dey fin' hit broke, dey fin' hit wasted. I try ter lib ter be er Leetle Sister er de Po', but I cain't, oh! I cain't!"

I tells her how I lub her, how ever'body lub her, but she shake her head. "Ef Jesus des lemme in, Mammy," she say, "I be happy in de lowes' place erroun' de throne. I wanter go, Mammy, ter be wid Jesus, ter be wid my farder, my mudder, wid Phil!" I knowed hit were comin'.

"Mammy," she say arter while, "talk ter me lack

I were er leetle chile ergin, don' stop. Po' ole Mammy! hol' me close twel dey comes fur me!"

Well, I gibs her wine, an' I talks an' talks, lack she tell me, all er-chokin', an' de tears des er-rinnin' down lack rain.

I thought I were hard, I thought I were cole, but I hain't ebber hab no tribberlatin' lack ter dis.

Well, I tells her 'bout Gord, lack she did n' know; I tells hit my way, de way she were borned ter, an' I says ober de ole hyme dat she uster lub, 'bout "He plant He footsteps in de sea, an' ride upon de storm," an' she smile 'ca'se she lack hit, but I dun know what ter do.

Bimeby de breaf git sof'er an' sof'er, an' she say, "Mammy, Mammy!" two er free times, an' I says, "Here Mammy, Baby," ever' time, an' she squiz my han' lack she lub me; den she retch out her arms an' smile. Hain't fur Mammy dis time, 'ca'se I knowed she seed 'em, 'ca'se I knowed she heared 'em call; 'pear lack de room was full er brightness an' de angils an' de light er Gord! Den I knowed fur sho' my Baby were gone, done gone fum dese ole arms fur ebber, done tuck de veil! Gone, ter sorrer an' ter triberlate no mo' on dis here yeth, whar dey hain't no war ner de breakin' er de hearts! Wid de promise

kep' an' de faith unbruk ; gone ter meet ole Marse
an' young Marse Phil! Nuffin' lef' at Brokenburne,
but de house an' de niggers, de home an' de sorrer!

We puts her ter sleep long sider young Marse
Phil, wid de roses an' vi'lets ober 'em. I ast hit
when dey kim ter me, an' ole Marse Phil he do
hit, 'dout er word, 'ca'se he know sumpen too, dat I
ain't know what.

De sun nebber shine de same sence den, an' de
years kim an' goes lack er holler horn. Hain't no
mo' joy dis sider dar,—dar whar de Baby sleeps.

Young Marse kim back arter de war were ober,
po', woun'ed, an' horngry,—mos' all de sodgers was
horngry,— an' we feeds er heap es dey passes.

Aaron see him comin', an' he rin ter de bed an' kiver
up he head; he des could n' b'ar hit, an' I hatter break
hit de bestes' I could.

He make me tell him all 'fore he eat, 'fore he res',
an' he cain't cry, but he git whiter an' whiter, an' he
eye git shinier an' shinier; den he laugh an' laugh,
an' rin ter de pianner an' play t'ings dat make de
very blood rin cole.

I don' t'ink as how he ebber plum unnerstan' hit,
but bimeby he git ca'mer, an' Aaron holp me git him

in de bed, an' we nuss an' feed him dar lack he were er baby.

My young Marse, dat lef' so proud, so gran', so mannish! When he git betterer, he ride erway suddent lack, 'douten er word errer "Good-bye."

He were gone er whole year, den he kim back suddent lack, lack he had n' been gone more 'n er day; dat de way he been er-doin' ebber sence.

Me an' Aaron rin de place an' keep hit comferble fur him when he kim, no matter de times er de day er night, an' don' 'pear ter take no notice.

Aaron mighty techy 'bout young Marse, an' don' wanter tell nuffin', he dat lack ole Marse.

Some folkes says young Marse crazy,— he hab ernough ter rin him crazy, Gord know!— but dey tells what is lies. Young Marse, lack me an' Aaron, des er-libin' in de pas', an' dar hain't no *now* fur we-all!

Brightly the sunlight gleamed upon the path of two early travelers, whose restless horses were waiting at the porch steps.

"Good-bye, Aunt Bene," one was saying, "I shall keep this rosebud always in memory of you and of your story."

"Good-bye, Aunt Bene," said the other, "I thank you for your kindness; should I have news of him in any way, I 'll certainly let you know."

Down through the winding walk of seeming dreamland, through the arch of roses, through the gateway, then, reluctantly, old Aaron gives up the horses.

"Young Marse's gues's mought 'bide twel young Marse kim," he complained. "'Spec's him home mos' any time, mought be ter-day!"

Being assured again that the departure was necessary, though much to be regretted, he made a most impressive farewell.

The travelers loitered, and nearly a quarter of a mile down the road, old Aaron came limping, running, panting, breathless.

"I furgit, young Marses," he gasped, "ter tell you 'bout de pedigree er dem dorgs an' hosses, but de breed er dem dorgs is powerful!"